Victoria 1000 X 5
Children's Book Recycling Project

<u>Did you know</u>? Creating the habit of nightly bedtime reading "adds up" to this: By the time your child enters school, he or she will hear stories from 1000 books or more! Read to your child each day and begin literacy development, a stronger connection to you, and a lifetime love of books.

Please accept this gift of a book as a reminder of the importance of reading to young children and help support our goal—that all children in Victoria will have at least a thousand books read to them before they enter Kindergarten.

The *Victoria "1000 X 5" Children's Book Recycling Project* is a partnership among Success by 6®, South Vancouver Island; Greater Victoria School District #61 and Saanich Neighbourhood Place.

GREAT LAKES &
RUGGED GROUND

Imagining Ontario

BY SARAH N. HARVEY & LESLIE BUFFAM
ILLUSTRATED BY KASIA CHARKO

ORCA BOOK PUBLISHERS

Deer, fish, saplings, corn.
The land gives everything.
Will its bounty last?

Furs traded for beads,
Radishes and gooseberries
Fill the ship *Nonsuch*.

Enough land for all.
A new life in a new place
And safety at last.

Are the dark woods safe?
The threat is real and too close.
She is not alone.

Locks open and close
With keys of stone and muscle.
No more portaging.

The mills are hungry.
Feed them pine trees, red and white.
Old growth gone for good.

Is it possible?
Tunnels carved through solid rock.
At last, Jackfish Bay.

Nickel, silver, gold.
Blasted from the earth, jingling
In pocket and purse.

Still lakes mirror a blaze
That does not burn. Paddles drip.
Stretch the blank canvas.

The men are at war.
Soft hands are strong and eager.
Hearth and home await.

Puck, pass, empty net.
Could this get any better?
He shoots! He scores! Yay!

A park is for all.
The pictographs are sacred.
Pink orchids are too.

In Moose Factory
They make hockey stars. *Wah-chay!*
The horseflies are huge.

North, south, east and west.
We make a place what it is.
Sing! Dance! Celebrate!

HISTORICAL NOTES

1. IROQUOIS OF THE EASTERN WOODLANDS

By the mid-1500s, up to 50,000 Haudenosaunee (People of the Longhouse), speaking different dialects of the Iroquoian language, lived among the hills and forests of southern Ontario. Villages, made up of longhouses built within palisade walls, were at the heart of their complex society. The "Three Sisters"—corn, beans and squash—allowed the Haudenosaunee to prosper. The women tended the crops, freeing the men for hunting, fishing, trapping, trading and fighting.

2. EUROPEAN CONTACT WITH FIRST NATIONS—1668-1670

Canadien explorers/fur traders moved westward and north seeking direct access to furs. When Radisson and des Groseilliers could not gain French support for their northern route, they sought and gained the support of English investors. In 1668, one ship, the *Nonsuch*, reached the shores of James Bay and overwintered. As the first of many English trips to Hudson Bay's shores, it marked the beginnings of the Hudson's Bay Company and English claims to this territory.

3. THE ARRIVAL OF THE LOYALISTS—1780s

In the early 1780s, Britain lost its American colonies. A diverse group of loyalists fled north to the shores of the St. Lawrence River and the Great Lakes. They were rewarded with grants of land and supplies. By 1791 the population had grown to more than 30,000. Unhappy under the regime of the Quebec government, the colonists asked for their own colony. In 1791 the British responded, creating the colonies of Upper and Lower Canada.

4. LAURA SECORD AND THE WAR OF 1812

In 1812, Canadians became embroiled in a war between Great Britain and the United States. An attack on Britain's North American colonies was seen as the fastest route to victory, but three years of fighting proved the Americans wrong. This difficult experience gave Upper Canadians both an identity and a sense of pride. Their colony would now be a staunchly conservative one, ready to do battle against the extreme democratic influences from south of the border.

5. STRENGTHENING THE COLONY—1830s

After the war, Upper Canadians worked to strengthen their colony. Construction began on the Rideau Canal; it was to provide a secure transportation route. Immigrants, many of them Irish, flocked to the colony and augmented the canal's French Canadian workforce. They helped carve the locks out of the untouched wilderness. Many never left the wilderness, felled either by accident or malaria. Opened in 1832, the canal fostered the development of the Ottawa Valley.

6. THE TIMBER TRADE IN THE OTTAWA VALLEY—1840s

The demand for squared timber changed the face of the Ottawa Valley. The red and white pine trees that fuelled the trade were so tall and tightly packed they blocked the sun. The rivers provided the means to transport the logs, and the Irish and French Canadian canal workers became the workforce. By the 1870s, mills began to appear to meet the demand for lumber, and these, in turn, brought more settlers to the region.

7. BUILDING THE RAILWAY—1880s

Railways changed the face of British North America, spurring economic and industrial growth. Where railways went, settlers and activity followed. Railway construction was also an integral part of Confederation. Building the all-Canadian route through the Precambrian shield was expensive and slow, but the need to suppress the Riel Rebellion in 1885 proved the railway's worth. In May 1885, Ontario's last spike was driven at Jackfish Bay.

8. MINING IN NORTHERN ONTARIO—1900s

At the turn of the century, railways continued to fuel economic and industrial expansion. As the tracks spread north, the "New Ontario" was discovered to hold a wealth of mineral resources. Nickel built Sudbury, silver spurred the growth of Cobalt, and gold created the growing community of Timmins. For a time, the Big Three gold mines—Hollinger, Dome and McIntyre—produced more gold than any other region in North America.

9. THE GROUP OF SEVEN—1920s

Throughout the 1920s and '30s, Ontario was at the heart of economic, lifestyle and cultural changes taking place throughout the nation. A distinctive Canadian style of painting, led by the Group of Seven, emerged. Their work focused on the Canadian landscape, in particular that of northern Ontario. The artists believed their art reflected the essence of the nation and guaranteed that Canada's image on the world stage would be identified with this region.

10. WORLD WAR II AND ONTARIO'S WOMEN—1940s

The outbreak of World War II saw men leave their jobs to join the armed forces. For the first time, married women with children were no longer confined to traditional roles. They joined the ranks of factory workers, assembling the items needed to support the war effort. Ontario's women demonstrated their strength and capability, but once the war ended, they were expected to, and did, return home.

11. THE TORONTO MAPLE LEAFS—1960s

Hockey has long been part of Ontario's sporting culture. During the early 1900s, amateur teams became professional and fierce rivalries were the norm. No rivalry was more intense than that between the Montreal Canadiens and the Toronto Maple Leafs. They fought some of their best hockey battles during the 1960s, with the Leafs emerging victorious as Stanley Cup champions four times. The Leafs' last victory in 1967 also heralded the end of the NHL Original Six.

12. ONTARIO'S ENVIRONMENTAL MOVEMENT—1980s

Over time, Ontario's citizens became aware that their industrial society was damaging the environment. Land, lakes and rivers were slowly being destroyed by the acid rain created by industrial waste and the phosphates produced by detergents. Something had to be done to avoid irreparable damage. Public pressure was applied. By the 1980s, Ontario led Canada in addressing environmental issues, including more than doubling the size of the province's park system.

13. TOURISM IN NORTHERN ONTARIO—1990s

In the 1980s there was a growing awareness that the resources of northern Ontario were fuelling the economy of the rest of the province, while the North was reaping few benefits. The Northern Ontario Heritage Fund was established to help develop and promote projects that would encourage tourism. Examples of the fund's success can be seen in two popular, award-winning destinations—Cochrane's Polar Bear Habitat and Heritage Village and Moose Factory's Cree Village Ecolodge.

14. MULTICULTURAL ONTARIO—2010

Immigrants and First Nations peoples have built the province of Ontario. In the 1960s, the federal and provincial governments enacted legislation to reduce discrimination. By the 1970s, immigrants made up 44 percent of Toronto's population, and state-supported multiculturalism recognized that their communities were essential to the province's cultural wealth. Toronto's Caribana celebrations provide an excellent example of Ontario's multicultural policy at work.

SEEK AND FIND!

1	cornhusk doll, papoose, bark canoes, longhouses, palisade walls, rabbit, coneflowers, white-tailed deer, blackberries, moose, wolf, scarlet tanager, pileated woodpecker, great blue heron, flying squirrels, maple leaves
2	des Groseilliers, *Nonsuch*, Red Ensign, children, papoose, fur pelts, iron kettles, blankets, tents, stockade, bark canoes, tundra swans, arctic hare, snow goose, Canada geese, arctic fox, mink, arctic wolf
3	log cabins, surveying tents, children, handsaw, bark canoes, cooking fires, washing line, deer, coyote, skunk, bald eagle, black bear, osprey, red fox, turkey, raccoon
4	six Iroquois warriors, Laura Secord, British soldier, tents, fireflies, horned owls, mouse, garter snake, moths, bats, wolf, birch trees, ferns
5	children, stonemasons, British soldiers, Colonel John By, lumberjacks, shanties, axes, Canada geese, salamander, ferns, trilliums, sparrow, raccoon, porcupine, warbler, chipmunk, skunk, moose
6	Union Jack, raft, loggers, children, axes, hand and crosscut saws, log chute, blue heron, gull, killdeer, bald eagle, mergansers, fish, loon
7	children, railway ties, shovel, horse, black bear, mountain lion, fish, bald eagle, crows, harrier hawk, Canada geese, terns, red-tailed hawk
8	children, shovels, pick-axes, washing line, barrel, miners' cabins, raccoon, coyote, black bear, crow, groundhog, robin, hare, hawk, blue jay, red fox
9	Arthur Lismer, Tom Thompson, puppy, water lilies, coneflowers, goldenrod, asters, snapping turtle, belted kingfisher, blue heron, dragonflies, scarlet tanager, blackbird, warbler, beaver, wolf
10	photographs, toolboxes, pliers, screwdrivers, war posters, lamps, head scarves, goggles, coveralls, overalls, cats, mice, mallet, supervisor
11	Tim Horton, Eddie Shack, hockey sticks, skates, Maple Leaf shirts, streamers, Montreal Canadien players, hats
12	canoes, dog, moose, woodpecker, scarlet tanager, yellow warbler, blue heron, Eastern bluebird, hare, garter snake, trilliums, turtle, blue flags, marsh marigolds, otter, bufflehead ducks, caribou, jack pine
13	Polar Bear Express, children, snowman, sleds, skates, hockey sticks, train trestle, snowy owls, arctic fox, arctic hares, caribou, snow geese
14	masqueraders, children, flags (Ontario, Canada, Franco-Ontario, and ten Caribbean nations), CN tower, sari

How many can you find?

Visit us at **www.imagining-ontario.ca** for more fun and facts!

Text copyright © 2010 Sarah N. Harvey and Leslie Buffam
Illustrations copyright © 2010 Kasia Charko

Library and Archives Canada Cataloguing in Publication

Harvey, Sarah N., 1950-
Great lakes & rugged ground : imagining Ontario / written by
Sarah N. Harvey and Leslie Buffam ; illustrated by Kasia Charko.

Issued also in an electronic format.
ISBN 978-1-55469-105-0

1. Ontario--History--Juvenile poetry. 2. Haiku, Canadian (English).
3. Children's poetry, Canadian (English). I. Buffam, Leslie II. Charko,
Kasia, 1949- III. Title. IV. Title: Great lakes and rugged ground.

PS8615.A764G74 2010   jc811'.6   C2010-903520-8

First published in the United States, 2010
Library of Congress Control Number: 2010928735

Summary: Ideally suited to young readers, *Great Lakes & Rugged Ground* provides an illustrated overview of the history of Ontario.

Mixed Sources
Cert no. SW-COC-001271
© 1996 FSC
FSC

Orca Book Publishers is dedicated to preserving the environment and has printed this book on paper certified by the Forest Stewardship Council.

Orca Book Publishers gratefully acknowledges the support for its publishing programs provided by the following agencies: the Government of Canada through the Canada Book Fund and the Canada Council for the Arts, and the Province of British Columbia through the BC Arts Council and the Book Publishing Tax Credit.

Cover artwork by Kasia Charko
Design by Teresa Bubela
Author photo by Dayle Sutherland

ORCA BOOK PUBLISHERS
PO Box 5626, STN. B
VICTORIA, BC CANADA
V8R 6S4

ORCA BOOK PUBLISHERS
PO Box 468
CUSTER, WA USA
98240-0468

www.orcabook.com
Printed and bound in Canada.

13 12 11 10 • 4 3 2 1